T0064684

G

The Story of a Madman

BY BILL EVANS

ARCHWAY
PUBLISHING

Archway Publishing books may be ordered through booksellers or by contacting:

Archway Publishing
1663 Liberty Drive
Bloomington, IN 47403
www.archwaypublishing.com
1 (888) 242-5904

ISBN: 978-1-4808-4931-0 (sc)
ISBN: 978-1-4808-4932-7 (e)

Library of Congress Control Number: 2017910817

Print information available on the last page.

Archway Publishing rev. date: 7/13/2017

FOREWORD

First of all, let me say that writing the Gregor series was fun and perhaps even liberating. As a writer, to be able to free yourself to say and write things that you dare not think or say in real life is perhaps the purest joy the art form of fiction has to offer. The journey that encompasses the writing of a fiction piece, whether it be a novel, novella, short story, or piece of flash fiction, is truly a marvel to any author. You begin the journey with perhaps a rough idea as to how to arrive at the finish line. But as any author will tell you, they are amazed at how they had gotten to the end. The ongoing construction that the mind induces is miraculous. An astonishing end to a tale is most probably more astonishing to the writer than to the amazed reader.

This was never more true than with the Gregor stories. The first of the series, titled "FRIENDS," was written as a flash fiction piece for *Alfred Hitchcock Mystery Magazine*. I had shown this piece to a few friends. They were blown away. Encouraged by this reaction, my next undertaking involved a follow-up titled "GREGOR." This drew an enthusiastic response from my inner circle of critics. They then queried about Gregor's beginnings. Relenting to their demands, "BABY G" came next, a prequel to the above stories. With a now mini-cult following asking and even demanding more Gregor, "PSYCHO G" was the logical conclusive piece to the Gregor saga. The problem was I couldn't stop writing. "PSYCHO G 2,3, and 4" manifested before my pen would rest. Each of the stories was written to stand on its own merits. The assemblage of the stories in Gregor's chronology seemed to work and make some sense. Thus I present you with the novella, *G: THE STORY OF A MADMAN*. Please enjoy, with my compliments.

Bill Evans
<u>wbillevans@aol.com</u>

BABY G

"I don't wanna wear baby shoes. I'm a big boy. I'm not a baby. I'm five."

"Shut the hell up," Gregor's father responded. He then took another swig from a bottle concealed by a brown paper bag. After scratching his stomach and then his crotch, the grizzled drunkard turned to the child and sneered.

"Be glad I don't dress you up like a little girl. Now wear the damn shoes. We can't afford new ones."

Gregor's lower lip jutted out as he sauntered out of the living room and away from his father. Although he was five years old, Gregor was very much undersized for his age. His tiny feet still fit into the baby shoes he had been wearing for over three years now. Well, he'd better get his little feet moving. He didn't want to get into any more trouble. Today he vowed to get to school on time for a change. Heading for the front door, Gregor heard his father shout something to him. He stopped to listen.

"One more thing," his dad snarled. "You'd better not shit yourself again today. It's bad enough that you're five years old and you still have to wear a diaper like a little baby. I'm tired of changing your shitty diaper. If you're such a big boy, then stop it. It's embarrassing. Now get to school."

"Okay, Daddy, I'll be a good boy." Gregor said this cheerfully. He wasn't angry at his father's words. Gregor never got angry.

The small child scampered happily out of the house and began his trek toward the schoolhouse. Most of the kids attending the small school took the school bus. Others were dropped off and picked up by parents or relatives, but not Gregor. He had to walk about a mile each way. He never complained.

Of course, coming home was always fun. He usually held out his arms and glided down like a hawk from atop the hillside where the school was perched. He sometimes imagined himself a superhero, saving the day. Some days he was an airplane, flying valiantly through the clouds. When he used his imagination, he always seemed to walk faster and get to places quicker. Getting home from school on time was usually not a concern. That was good because he didn't like getting into trouble.

It was getting to school that was a problem. He was almost always late. Climbing the steep hillside while hurriedly winding his little feet through the maze of narrow concrete streets was exhausting. He had been a frail, sickly child for most of his life. But he never used it as an excuse. He was a happy child. He was a good boy.

On Kearsarge Street, about a block from the school, Gregor stopped suddenly. He stood there for about thirty seconds, standing perfectly still while grunting. He looked at his expression in the reflection on a nearby car window. His face was agitated and contorted. Then it occurred to him. He had pooped his pants again. He decided he wouldn't tell anyone. If anyone asked, he'd deny it. Gregor was always frustrated after he pooped his pants.

"I hate my butt," he muttered quietly to himself. Then the child quickly forgave himself. The frustration, just like any other emotion, never lasted long with Gregor.

This happy boy skipped merrily the rest of the way to his school and quietly entered the main building leading to the classrooms. He cautiously tiptoed down the dark, vacant marble hallways. He was late again. He would be in trouble again. Gregor didn't like being in trouble. He was a good boy.

As he entered his kindergarten classroom, the other kids almost immediately began giggling and holding their noses. Gregor immediately went over to his assigned group table and took his seat. As he did so, the other four children at the table rose and fled as if Gregor had some kind of terrible disease. They made quite a ruckus, which disrupted the art activity happening at the time. Amid the clamor, paint was spilled all over an adjoining table, and two children began crying.

Everyone was looking at Gregor. He didn't care. He stopped caring about things like this a long time ago. And he was glad the others left his table. Now he could spread out and do his work with more space available.

The teacher, Mrs. Kindred, calmly and professionally quieted the children and quickly restored order. She then discreetly sauntered over to Gregor's table.

"Gregor, I think maybe you have to go potty," she whispered.

"No, I don't have to," Gregor protested.

"Gregor, maybe you made poopies in your diaper. C'mon, I'll change you."

"I don't have to," Gregor shouted in an agitated voice. He then tried to ignore the teacher and began the painting activity.

The teacher calmly yet assertively took Gregor by the hand and led him to the bathroom. She swiftly and expertly changed his diaper. Gregor didn't resist. He was glad. He felt much better.

Gregor returned to the classroom amid squealing laughter. The other children whispered to each other while pointing at Gregor. He calmly proceeded to his table, unaffected by the others. He didn't need or require their approval. He simply felt nothing.

It was time to do a clay-shaping activity. Gregor had been labeled as "noncreative" by his teacher. He knew this because he had overheard her tell the principal this information and much more.

Oh, Gregor was plenty creative. The world was not ready for his creativity—not yet. Everyone would discover his talents soon enough. He knew this even at a young age. You see, Gregor was an old soul. Besides, the stuff he would make with the clay would just frighten everyone anyhow. The world wasn't ready for Gregor's creativity. So he would simply fashion yet another ashtray out of the clay as he had always done.

Gregor liked being at school. He felt safe there. He almost never got into trouble. Besides, he could always count on eating a good lunch at the school. Sometimes this would be the only meal he'd eat all day.

The annoying part of school was that from time to time, they would ask Gregor to visit with a special doctor. The doctor would ask really silly questions. Gregor usually wouldn't answer right away in hopes that it would discourage her. They made him take tests. The doctor suspected Gregor had abnormal brain dysfunction. Gregor made sure they would never be able to prove that. He would probably get into trouble if they truly knew what he was thinking all the time. So he would eventually answer the opposite thing he thought when given a question to answer. This confused the doctor. Nobody would ever catch on. He was too smart. Playing dumb was usually a very smart thing to do.

This school day ended all too quickly, and Gregor headed home with the usual trepidation. His father would be waiting. His dad never seemed to approve of anything he did and blamed him for things that weren't his fault. No matter the circumstance, Gregor always seemed to land in trouble. He didn't like to be in trouble. It wasn't fair.

Gregor decided not to dwell on this. It was impossible for him to have negative feelings about anything. He was such a good boy. The child skipped and hummed and laughed and sang to himself as he wound his way through the maze of streets that led down to his family residence. Yes, Gregor loved his dad and his friends and his teacher. He loved everybody. He was a good boy who wouldn't harm a fly. He picked up the pace so he would get home quicker.

Gregor thought he saw a small black cloud moving around on a broken piece of sidewalk across from where he was skipping. Out of curiosity, he moved closer to inspect this movement. It was a large school of black ants, busily moving about on the broken concrete and loose dirt underneath. Gregor sat down next to the curb and studied them intently. He was captivated. He gazed in wonderment at the industrial and methodical actions of the insects. Each worker seemed to know and understand his role. They busily carried, constructed, and built, with each individual ant working in unison with the others. They all worked in beautiful, systematic orchestration. How did they each know what to do?

Gregor lost track of time. He did this often, which generally landed him in hot water. He stood up and yawned. He waved good-bye to the ant friends and scampered away. He'd better get home soon. Gregor began humming his favorite tune but then suddenly stopped in his tracks. Something had just occurred to him, and Gregor broke out into a large grin that made his face glow like an angel. Full of glee, Gregor skipped back to the ant colony. With a controlled frenzy, Gregor savagely leaped onto the horde of ants and began stomping viciously on them. The panicked ants scurried everywhere as Gregor continued stomping while cackling with wide-eyed excitement. Hundreds of ants laid still as the enraged child continued to seek and destroy any remnants of the colony that remained alive. Yeah, sure, some of them escaped. But Gregor was certain he had gotten most of them. Gregor swelled with pride. He had done a good job.

Gregor was a bit weary from the excessive physical exertion he had to perform on the ants. After the busy day at school with limited physical nourishment, the child needed to rest. He sat down on the curb and leaned on a nearby fire hydrant. The small child fell fast asleep.

When he awoke, Gregor found himself seated in the middle of a sandbox. He was at the park. How did that happen? This wasn't the first time he'd found himself somewhere and couldn't explain how he'd gotten there. He hated when this happened, and he then felt a sudden surge of panic. His father would be furious. He would be accused of not paying attention again. None of this was his fault.

Just like every other emotion, the panic soon faded away. Okay, so he was at the park. It was very late. He was going to get into trouble anyhow. The child figured he might as well stay for a while and enjoy himself.

It was getting dark. After carefully and meticulously crafting an elaborate castle in the sand, it was time to leave. Gregor stepped out of the sandbox to admire his work. The multi-level castle was replete with a moat, a tall tower, and a drawbridge. This was the kind of skill and craftsmanship he dared not show at school. No one knew he was a genius. This was a secret Gregor kept to himself.

Gregor just had to get home now. It was so very late. As he turned to walk away, an unprovoked fury engulfed him. He turned and dove back into the sandbox.

"I'm a giant. You must all die," he screamed. In a berserker-like frenzy, he began bashing the castle to smithereens. Gregor's face was aglow as he completed the demolition and carefully smoothed over the sand's surface. Upon inspection of the contents in the sandbox, Gregor seemed satisfied and was now truly ready to trek homeward. Finally!

But wait, what was that? Gregor turned his head sharply to the left. Was he mistaken or did something move? He could have sworn he had just seen a man in a green pea coat disappear behind the monkey bars. Oh, it was late. Surely the boy's eyes were playing tricks on him again. But just as a safeguard, Gregor positioned himself better to see the area around the monkey bars. The man would surely reappear on the other side of the bars. If there was a man. But no one showed up on the other side. Was the man hiding?

Gregor waited and waited. Nothing. Where did this guy go? Now he was scared.

Gregor's natural curiosity got the best of him, and he decided to investigate further. He tentatively crept toward the area where the man had disappeared. The boy looked all around and found nothing. With a sigh of relief, he backed up a few steps and shrugged his shoulders. Did Gregor truly imagine seeing the ominous figure? This was puzzling, but Gregor could ill afford to waste any more time worrying about it. He was going to be in so much trouble that he'd probably be grounded for a week. He had to leave now. Without looking, Gregor pivoted 180 degrees and sprinted right into—

Gregor gasped in startled fright. He collided directly into the man with the green coat. Gregor fell awkwardly to the ground. The mysterious man had been standing quietly behind him for some minutes now, grinning a sinister, toothy smile. Rather than scramble back to his feet, Gregor just laid there in stunned silence, his mouth hanging open in paralyzing fear.

"Hi, little guy. Don't be alarmed. I'm harmless, really. By the way, what's up with the baby shoes?"

"Don't tease me," Gregor admonished. "I'm a big boy."

"Why, yes—yes of course you are. No offense intended."

The man in the green pea coat had an engaging smile. It put the boy at ease. Gregor decided he wasn't going to be afraid of the stranger anymore. The man sensed this and felt encouraged to keep the conversation going with the child.

"Please allow me to introduce myself. My name is Greenman. Donald Greenman, prognosticator for the pungent, perpetuator of the pragmatic, solution solver of the forgotten and forsaken—at your service."

Gregor was confused by the slick-talking stranger. This guy was trying to be scary. *Allow the fear*, Gregor thought. The boy wanted to taste the fear, to savor it, to relish in its energy. The problem was Gregor just couldn't muster up any emotion at all—even now. He was disappointed that he didn't have the ability to feel things, at least not for very long.

"My name is Gregor," the child managed to stammer from a quaking voice. Maybe there was a bit of tension in his voice after all. Maybe there was still hope for Gregor. Maybe he could feel this tension, and perhaps use it to tap other dormant emotions lying deep under the surface. No, that was wishful thinking. He would never have that caring thing that others had. But for now, he clung to this little bit of tension that had somehow infiltrated his system. He would relish it for now. Gregor knew that it too would soon subside.

"Well, salutations, my young friend. Again, my name is Donald. Donald Greenman."

"Nice to meet you Green Man," Gregor replied meekly.

Green Man erupted with laughter.

"Why are you here, Green Man?" The child realized that perhaps that was too bold a question to ask. The stranger responded almost immediately.

"Surely you know why I'm here, little man. I'm a genie, sort of. I'm here to grant you a wish. Your wish is my command."

Gregor pondered this for a minute. If only it were true. But magic genies were make-believe. They weren't real, and he told Green Man so.

"I'm far from make-believe, as you can see. So just go ahead and try me. What do you have to lose? Name your wish, and I'll make it come true. Trust me."

This got Gregor thinking. He was always in trouble with his family. He wished that he wouldn't get into trouble with then anymore. He told this to Green Man.

"Well, I can make your wish come true little man. Are you sure that you want this request to be your wish?"

Gregor contemplated this deeply. As the boy was thinking, Green Man said as an aside. "But be advised child. If that is what you wish, I'll grant it. But remember-I always finish what I start."

FRIENDS

"Jack-o'-lantern, jack-o'-lantern, you are such a funny sight,
As you sit there in the cow field looking out at the night"
The seven-year-old sang innocently while sitting in the hayloft in the barn.

"You are a sweet child, with the voice of an angel."

Gregor looked up at his Auntie Jen and smiled like a glowing cherub. Auntie Jen smiled back, her heavily lined face weary from decades of back-breaking farm work. Only she and the boy were left after the rest of the family was murdered by the heinous serial killer know as Green Man. The boy witnessed it all, but it seemingly had little effect on him. Auntie Jen would do her best to raise the boy to manhood.

"Gregor, I must get back to work. But tell me, we are missing another chicken from the coop. Have you seen it?"

"No Auntie Jen," the boy replied dryly. "They are my friends; I would never harm them."

Auntie Jen looked confused, then shrugged. She reminded the boy that lunchtime was about an hour away and then departed. The boy calmly climbed from the loft and entered the coop as he had done each day since the murders. Amidst the clamor and squawking, Gregor carefully selected a fine hen from the wired confines of the coop. With great pomp and presence, the boy carried the panicked bird to the "altar." He ceremoniously raised the cackling hen overhead and violently bashed it against the jagged rocks. The small child laughed heartily as the bloodied chicken raced around the barn until finally falling over, limp and lifeless. Upon opening the barn gate, Gregor carried the carefully wrapped hen out to the field, being sure not to trip over the numerous pumpkins which littered the pasture. Taking his little toy shovel from his rear pocket, the child carefully dug a neat grave in the soft soil and gently laid the hen to rest. One of the nearby pumpkins was rolled onto the grave, to be used as yet another burial marker.

"Another of my friends is now safe," the boy muttered as Auntie Jen rang the cowbell summoning Gregor to lunch.

"You were once a yellow pumpkin, growing on a sturdy vine,
Now you are a jack-o'-lantern, see your candlelight shine,"

The boy hummed as he trod to the farmhouse. It was important for the child to finish the song he had started earlier. Yes, from now on, Gregor would always finish everything he started.

GREGOR

He stood silently by the window, as he did every night, peering out at the masses being bathed by the blinking neon as they hustled and shuffled along the busy midtown Manhattan street below. The sounds of cabbies honking, vendors shouting, and police whistles blowing was a stark change from the quiet and serene Iowa farmland whence he came. But that was in the past. He was here now in New York City, with all of its crowding, cluster, and glorious decadence. As he looked down, it seemed as if the buildings, the throngs of people, the street barricades, the signs, everything was one on top of the other. There was not enough room. It was smothering. All life, all decency, was being snuffed out by a pernicious cloud of uncaring that pervaded every person and every "thing." With all of its faults, and all of its evils—here he was in NYC. It was his city. This was home now. And, although he was repulsed, Gregor had never felt more alive.

Gregor was unsettled, but that would soon change. He hadn't made any friends yet. Gregor was the kind of guy who needed friends. That would happen in due time. First, he needed a place to live. Upon arriving in NYC, it was decided that he would rent a small flat in the heart of the Broadway district. There would always be interesting people in that part of town. He settled on a small one-bedroom, one-bath apartment on the third floor of a run-down building on Forty-Third Street. The first floor of the building had a deli storefront on the left and an Irish pub on the right. The narrow, dimly lit entrance between the two led to a grimy lobby. A shabby spiraling staircase with broken and missing handrails was the lone access point up to the run-down apartments.

When he saw it, his heartbeat quickened. He immediately knew apartment 3A would do fine. The rental agent had shown the apartment hurriedly. These agents were always so very busy. She also tried to gloss over many of the imperfections. Gregor could live with the noise, the faulty wiring, the corroded pipes. Perhaps the biggest drawback, most notably, was a rather plump rat with an exceptionally long tail, lurking in the shadows of a corner in the bedroom. The agent seemed not to notice. Gregor didn't mind.

The assimilation to NYC life over the next few weeks went smoothly. The deli downstairs agreed to receive Gregor's mail. Any trash to be thrown away was mixed in with garbage cans that the pub set out on the curb every Tuesday morning. Even Gregor's roommate would not be a problem. He decided he would get along famously with the rat. This would not be difficult. After all, Gregor had many friends on the farm. Of course, those friends were farm animals—mostly chickens. Sadly, those friends had passed on. Gregor needed a new friend. The rat would do just fine.

On Gregor's eighteenth birthday, it dawned on him that he was a man. It was time for him to leave. No, it was time to escape. Yes, escape the farmland. He had fond memories of the farm, of all his friends, and of Auntie Jen. What happened to Auntie Jen was a shame. There she was one day, just hanging there in the rafters of the large, drafty barn. What an ignoble way to die! Gregor had discovered her there much to his horror. The local sheriff quickly assumed she had done this to herself. That "local yokel," as Gregor liked to describe the police, was clueless. He didn't seem to know much about police work. Heck, he didn't know enough to come in out of the rain, as far as Gregor was concerned. The official ruling that later came out was that Auntie Jen had died of an apparent suicide. The ruling was laughable. Gregor knew better.

It was time to vacate the life he had known for over a decade. Obviously the serial killer known as Green Man would soon be stalking Gregor. The killer had taken everything and everyone of importance. Now the killer would finally come for him. Gregor needed a place to escape, a new city where no one knew him. It would have to be a city where anyone could just blend in, become anonymous, unobserved, and obscure. He was older now. He was truly ready to begin anew. A new city. A new career.

With a large inheritance from Auntie Jen and the sale of the farm, Gregor found himself "well off." He could easily afford the smallish apartment in NYC. It was comfortable enough and had the built in perk of providing a "friend" with whom he would reside. The location was perfect too, in that he could stand next to the window and peer unobserved at the masses below. Gregor was very happy.

Over the next few weeks, Gregor developed a daily routine. Of course, this was important. How would one maintain one's sanity without routine? Promptly at 6:15, Gregor commenced with the usual scattering of a few potato chips in the middle of the living room floor. Within minutes, the rat would emerge from some shadowy obscured crevice in the corner of the room. The fat gray rodent wobbled cautiously toward the chips, always stopping every few steps to raise his snout and sniff for any danger. Gregor stood perfectly still next to the curtains and dared not move, lest he frighten his friend away. Gregor found pride in himself and a connectivity to the rat each evening as his friend nibbled on his salty dinner. Gregor hoped the rat would learn to like him, and perhaps even depend on him. True friends needed and depended on each other.

Each day the rat became more emboldened and less cautious when coming out for his evening treat. A bond was forming. A trust. This suited Gregor just fine.

While standing perfectly still as per his custom each evening, this particular evening would be delightfully different. Gregor noticed a light snap on out of the corner of his eye. Turning his head slowly and deliberately, so as not to alarm his feasting friend, Gregor sought out the source of the distraction. That's when he noticed a corner apartment across the street and diagonal from Gregor's residence. It was truly a miracle that he was able to observe this fortunate event amidst all of the glitter and visual noise permeating NYC.

What had caught his eye was a thirty-ish woman in a pink satin sleeveless nightgown, walking and pausing by the large plate-glass apartment window. She was oblivious to the possibility that anyone could possibly be watching her. Gregor's mouth hung open in astonishment. She looked like a model from an Edward Hopper painting. Gregor felt a strange tingling down below. How thrilling it was, to be able to intrude on someone without being observed. What a great stroke of good fortune. Perhaps she could be yet another friend. How marvelously exhilarating!

The new routine had been delightfully established. After providing dinner for his friend each evening, Gregor would stand promptly at 6:00 p.m. by the window curtains. The rat would saunter out and begin his feast at about 6:15. And then, right on cue at 6:45, the light would flip on. The woman from across the street would appear innocuously through the window of her apartment. Gregor would often strain his eyes in an attempt to more clearly distinguish her features, but this proved difficult. She might be pretty, but Gregor was unsure about that. He thought about getting a telescope or binoculars, but immediately reprimanded himself for having such thoughts. Only Peeping Toms would do such a thing. He was a good boy.

Gregor spent the next day walking around town. First, Park Avenue down to Thirty-First Street, then over to Fifth Ave and back up to Forty-Third again. Over and over he did this, with a warm smile on his face. He just blended in as he moved with the hordes of scurrying people busily heading in all directions. Integrating himself in the crowd gave Gregor a feeling of belonging. He felt safe.

Evening was fast approaching, and Gregor had to get back. He so looked forward to his usual evening activity. Today was going to be just a bit different, however. He had a special surprise planned for his roommate. Gregor hoped the furry friend would appreciate it.

As he trudged up the three flights of steps leading to the apartment, Gregor eagerly reached into the brown paper sack that he had been holding for hours. Earlier he had purchased a pair of heavy leather gloves and a beautifully ornate paperweight—the kind that made snowflakes when shaken. After removing the items from the bag, he placed them carefully on the kitchen counter. Meticulously, the kitchen cabinet was opened, and three large, salty and greasy potato chips were removed from the container inside. The chips were then laid carefully in a row on the floor. They were placed in an area of the living room a bit more centrally located than usual. This was necessary, as Gregor required some room for error.

Gregor quietly retrieved the gloves and paperweight and moved stealthily over to his usual spot by the window. He gingerly snapped the gloves onto each hand and then carefully and slowly placed the paperweight into his outer jacket pocket. He then stood perfectly still. Nothing happened for about twenty minutes. Then, right on cue, the rat appeared. He stood on his hind legs in the corner and didn't move. His yellow eyes seemed to be fixated on Gregor. Did he suspect something unusual going on? The rat's instincts seemed to be on full alert. "So the game is afoot," Gregor muttered silently as he nearly squealed aloud with delight.

Eventually, hunger gave way to caution, and with trepidation the rat began to move slowly toward the chips.

Just then, the light switched on at the apartment across the street. Was it 6:45 already? It was his other friend, the female friend. There she was in her usual satin slip, only this time it was blue. My, how the pale blue set off her auburn hair nicely. Gregor seemed transfixed as he stared unblinkingly, watching his neighbor dart around her apartment gracefully as if walking on air. When this woman moved, she just seemed to glide like a fairy princess. Maybe she was a professional dancer; who knew? But, *Oh my, so refined and elegant,* thought Gregor. The sight of her always made his heart flutter. A warm feeling engulfed Gregor. He felt blessed. It just now dawned on him that he had not only one but two very good friends. Gregor decided a long time ago that standards should always be set when friendships are formed. These friends had all of the outstanding traits that were required, perhaps even demanded by Gregor. Yes, these friends met the standard and were exemplary. Both of them were consistent, on-time, and reliable. This was important. So very important.

Gregor had been distracted by the woman and reminded himself that he must now get on with the task at hand. Gregor had remained motionless so as not to alarm his roommate. The rat seemed to be more emboldened and careless as he settled into the daily routine. That was good. It was imperative that the rat be as comfortable as possible, and not be alarmed by Gregor's presence. The rat finally made it to the chips and began greedily feasting on its dinner, totally oblivious to its surroundings. "Eat heartily, my friend," Gregor mumbled. The rat was not alarmed by the sound of his voice. This brought a sly grin to Gregor's face.

Gregor turned his attention back to the woman. She darted in and out of view, briskly moving about. One never knew when she would again appear into view. Gregor would wait with eager anticipation at the thought that she might reappear at any moment. She was teasing him. He liked that.

Although he was inwardly turbulent with pulsating exhilaration, Gregor stayed outwardly calm as usual. In a very slow, deliberate, even tedious manner, Gregor reached into his side pocket and pulled out the paperweight. His timing was perfect, as his furry roommate had just finished with his dinner. The rat very casually turned and began to waddle away toward the baseboard in the shadowy corner. Gregor suddenly sprung with cat-like quickness, whirled and launched the glass sphere at the unsuspecting rat. With a sickening crunch, the weight found its mark as it violently struck the back of the skull of the plump rodent. A horrifying high pitched squeal belched from the rat as it lay squirming and spastic. Gregor hurriedly pounced on the injured and stunned animal. He held it up triumphantly and immediately inspected the creature closely and with great care. He had not killed his friend. Gregor giggled with uncontrolled excitement.

Holding the rat in his gloved hands, Gregor shook it vigorously in an attempt to coax it back to consciousness. As the rat began to regain its senses, it instinctively panicked and began whipping its long tail against the padded gloves. The animal tried to fight, as it bit viciously at the iron-gripped hands behind the leather gloves. Gregor's eyes opened wide with pleasant surprise, and he began to cackle with exuberant glee. His furry friend had not let him down. Gregor was afraid that his friend would not rise up to meet the challenge. To Gregor's admiration and delight, the rat had come through with flying colors.

The struggling rat continued its frenzied biting, baring its uneven green teeth like a rabid dog, gnawing violently against the heavy leather. After about ten minutes of this unbridled glee, Gregor noticed that the rat was slowing down. It then just suddenly stopped, probably due to a combination of exhaustion and a recognition as to its fate. Gregor disappointedly held the rat up to face level and stared into its bloodshot and hazy yellow eyes. The rat just hung there limply as it stared back in terror.

Gregor decided to make one more attempt to prompt the rat into action. This evening's festivities had been so much fun. There was no need to end things so early. Surely the rat understood that. To Gregor's dismay, however, his captive did not cooperate. After being shaken vigorously for about thirty seconds, it was obvious that the limp unresponsive rodent had no more fight left in it. Gregor felt himself getting angry. No, not angry. Gregor never got angry. He decided that *frustration* was a better word. Yes, he was frustrated. He held the rat by the neck and began to slowly squeeze.

His victim's eyes widened in horror as the gloved hands slowly tightened around the thin tiny gray neck. Slowly, continually, painfully, the pressure increased. In a futile last-ditch attempt at preservation, the rat nibbled sluggishly at the bent knuckle closest to its gaping mouth. Its little legs flailed around in a panicked attempt to gain some semblance of leverage or balance. This final surge of desperation soon ended, as the rat once again just hung limply in its master's vice-like grip. The rat just simply quit. Maybe it was because of a fatalistic resignation to its fate. Regardless, the battle was over.

Gregor yanked the rat up to face level and peered deep into its eyes. He saw defeat and dread. This excited Gregor and prompted him to continue squeezing with more and more pressure. The rat's eyes began to bulge bigger and bigger, as the pressure mounted. Gregor screamed like a berserker warrior, and with a final suffocating squeeze, *pop,* the rat's head exploded like a grenade. Blood, tiny bone fragments, and eye fluid spurted in all directions. Gregor's face and mouth were blanketed with the gooey, sticky body liquid. Gregor licked away the debris on his lips as he smiled and giggled maniacally.

He held what was left of his friend close to him. Determined not to let the fun end just yet, Gregor began dancing with his limp companion, serenading and waltzing across the dining room floor. Pivoting and sashaying, Gregor imagined himself in an eighteenth-century English castle. Yes, he was royalty. Perhaps a duke. Maybe a prince. Yes, a prince with a lavish princess at his side. The coronets were blaring as multicolored perfumed flowers showered down onto the dance hall, with his princely court smiling and nodding in approval. This was such a magical evening.

As the evening wore on, Gregor grew weary. He dropped the dead rat onto the floor and then carefully stepped over its limp lifeless body so as not to desecrate the corpse. "Poor little guy," Gregor mumbled. Gregor immediately decided he would do the right thing. He would give his friend a proper burial. It's a shame he didn't have a name for his friend. It had died anonymously, ignobly. He had to make amends for this oversight and make sure it didn't happen again.

It was still hard to believe that it had been a full twenty-four hours since his roommate had passed. Although he was in mourning, Gregor decided that it was best to get back into a routine as soon as possible. His friend had died, and Gregor would need to grieve properly. And he would. But mental stability was important to Gregor. There would be a proper burial, of course, and a tombstone. But was that really necessary? After all, the rat died nameless. What would be inscribed on the stone? The rat certainly didn't need a tombstone. Not now, especially not now that he was safe. Gregor felt a little bit of jealousy, but only for a second. The rat had it easy. Now he was safely at rest. The road destiny had selected for Gregor would be much more difficult. He decided that his lot had been cast, and he had to deal with it.

He had decided her name would be Margo. Yes. The name fit her beautifully. Gregor stood by the curtains in mesmerized amazement as she flittered around her apartment. A new routine was in full implementation, and it would necessarily center on Margo. She would now get most of his attention. In a weird way, she was all that he had left.

Gregor stood by the curtains for many hours. In fact, he stood there much longer than usual. He didn't want to leave Margo. He missed his roommate. Why did he have to die? Why do things always have to change? It seemed unfair that it was he, Gregor, who always had to adjust. Everyone else seemed to have it so easy.

Feeling full of self-pity and weariness, Gregor slumped down to the floor. He would rest for a few moments and collect himself. He began to sob.

Gregor awoke suddenly. Damn, he had fallen asleep. Wait a minute—where was he? This was not his apartment. Confused, and not fully awake, Gregor scrambled to his feet. He mysteriously found himself in a dusty and dimly lit hallway. It was adorned in a seventies-style decor, with cracked "mellow yellow" walls and an overly worn psychedelic-colored rainbow carpet. This hallway was different. It definitely was not the building where he resided. The hallway was dark and musty, with a lightbulb in a nearby fixture that flickered off and on, and Gregor was startled by the ominous shadows that were cast all around him. He let out a mild shriek that sounded a bit insincere in Gregor's mind. It almost sounded like he was gurgling with mouthwash after having brushed his teeth. Gregor chuckled at the thought. He had a strange way of reacting to danger.

"No more jokes," he said to himself in a scolding manner. There was work to be done. He was a problem solver. And, as was Gregor's strength, he didn't allow adversity to affect him very long. Gregor had always had a knack for turning terror into amusement, and he soon found himself giggling at the now seemingly comical characters dancing rhythmically on the long walls. He always tried to look at things positively. And my how Gregor had an imagination!

Even though he now felt somewhat relaxed, Gregor knew at once that it was imperative that he leave this building. After all, here he was in a strange place, with no explanation as to how he had gotten here. He probably should have been alarmed, but he wasn't. He wasn't about to panic. After all, this was not the first time something like this had happened. Gregor had always figured out what to do in the past. He would work himself out of this jam too. If he could just focus. "Concentrate Gregor, concentrate," he said, trying to be serious. He couldn't stop giggling.

After regaining a modicum of composure, Gregor slowly and calmly walked to the end of the hallway and pulled on the door marked "exit." The rusted metallic fire door didn't open. Adrenaline surged through Gregor's veins as he pulled more strongly. The exit door wasn't going to budge.

"Okay, so no need to panic. Come on G, think!" He giggled at his remark. That was the first time he had ever referred to himself by his first initial. He liked it. He would do it again some time.

Just then he heard it. *Clomp* and then *clomp* again. Then it stopped. It was someone wearing hard shoes, perhaps high-heeled shoes, walking on a solid wooden floor just behind the locked hallway exit door. Then he heard it again—*clomp ... clomp ... clomp*—slowly, meticulously, in a calculated way coming closer. Gregor was now breathing heavily. Who was it? What did they want?

Then the thought struck him. "OMG, it's Margo!" he shrieked. He then lowered his voice but continued the self-talk. "I must be in her building. Oh, heavens, she mustn't see me here. She'll think I'm some kind of stalker—a pervert perhaps. Oh, no. She mustn't find me here."

Gregor stood completely still and listened closely. The steps resumed, getting closer and closer—*clomp ... clomp ... clomp.* Whoever it was, they were now standing just on the other side of the door. Then a horrifying thought struck Gregor. Maybe it wasn't Margo after all. Could it be Green Man? Did he lure me here to finally exterminate me? Gregor, the only surviving member of his family, was the last of the serial killer's unfinished business.

Gregor couldn't scream or call for help. He was paralyzed, his vocal cords frozen with fear. Whoever was behind the door was hesitating before opening it. Why didn't they come through? *Why torture me and keep me in suspense?* he thought. Then it dawned on Gregor. If he were a serial killer, he would behave in the exact same manner.

Gregor immediately began to calm down. He never stayed frightened for too long about anything, even the prospect of facing the notorious and ruthless Green Man.

So Gregor just sat down and smirked and waited. Soon the door would open. Whoever was behind the door would present themselves soon enough. And Gregor would deal with it—as he had always done. Yes, Gregor would keep the promise he had made to himself when he was seven years old. This was an important promise. Gregor would always finish what he had started.

PSYCHO G

(PART 1)

An overpowering stench of disinfectant and bleach permeated the air as the fluorescent lights beat down upon the occupants of the psych ward, robbing them of life, and will, and dignity. Some of the gown-clad psychiatric patients walked zombie-like up and down the sterile marble hallway on the west wing of Floor 7A. Others just sat around in the rec room, staring blankly at the white-washed walls. There was no thinking, no feeling, and no hope. 7A was a kind of purgatory—a void, a soulless existence.

None of this ever affected Gregor. He was a veteran of the psych units and had the system all figured out. He was too smart for them. He often mused to himself that he was even too smart for his own good. While acknowledging this, Gregor could honestly say that he had few regrets in his sixty years on this planet.

Gregor stooped over his small, unbreakable plastic mirror to more closely examine his greying temples and wrinkled face. "Where have the years gone?" he mumbled to himself. He didn't really mean those words because, frankly, he just didn't really care. It was something people say, so he thought he'd say it. Gregor never worried about much, especially about things out of his control.

Today he was scheduled to be released from the psych unit. They never kept him for long. Sometimes it was for seven days. Other times, it was for about a month or so. It was never longer than that. After each 303 hearing, he would be stamped as psychologically fit to rejoin society. During the hearings, the board of psychologists would ask him a litany of silly questions. Gregor always deceived them. They tried to peer into his soul, but Gregor would not allow it. Oh, the books they could write and the lectures they could give if Gregor would just give them a glimpse of what was going on inside. But they didn't know. They would never truly know.ll

---

Ever since he was five years old and informally diagnosed as having "abnormal brain dysfunction," Gregor had been on the defensive. One time—and only one time—he had made the mistake of letting his guard down. Gregor was eighteen at the time and living in New York City. While there, he applied for an insurance sales position. A person could blend in with a job like that and make lots of friends. Gregor didn't have many friends, and for some inexplicable reason, the friendships never lasted very long. Gregor applied for the job. The company asked him to take a standard psychological test similar to the MMPI exam. The test measured personality traits. Gregor was curious himself and took the test gladly. He wondered if he had that salesman's personality required for the job. Much to the surprise and horror of everyone, he was diagnosed as having the personality of a "full-fledged psychopath, with a tendency of sporadic paranoia." Luckily, these results were not allowed to be shared with anyone. Federal laws and regulations saw to that. Gregor was relieved. He vowed to never answer such questions honestly ever again. And he never did.

The staff on 7A wished Gregor well as he was being released from confinement. At the present time, the gang on 7A were the only friends Gregor had in this world. The pudgy nurse everyone called Nurse Crotchet was especially kind to Gregor. Her heartfelt good-bye touched Gregor, sort of. At least he thought he should somehow be touched by her compassion. Regardless, Gregor knew how to play the part. He acted all sultry and emotional as he exited through the security gate that screened the psych patients from the hospital's general population. Gregor had a hard time connecting with emotions. His entire family and many close friends had been murdered by the sinister serial killer known only to authorities as "Green Man." After all of these atrocities had occurred, something in Gregor had died too.

The elevator doors slammed shut, and the newly released patient sped downward in the smallish elevator. Gregor started to sweat. He felt claustrophobic and panicky in the confines of this iron monster. In what was just a matter of seconds, but seemed much longer, the elevator doors finally opened with a hiss. The monster spat its lone occupant out into the main lobby of the hospital. Gregor took two steps forward and then turned abruptly. His chest was tightening, his breathing short and rapid. Gregor was in the throes of a full-scale panic attack. He scurried to re-enter the elevator. Too late! The doors quickly closed as if anticipating his move. In a frenzy, Gregor pounded on them, pleading with them to open. His efforts proved futile. He wanted to go back upstairs. He didn't feel safe. Gregor just stood there and sobbed like a newborn infant.

Gregor quickly regained his composure, just like he always did. He calmed himself as he looked around. After locating the nearest restroom, Gregor quietly—and without alarming anyone's suspicions—entered the nearest stall and fished out a set of scrubs that he had hidden in his travel bag. After dressing, Gregor headed to the admissions desk in the lobby. He informed the wide-eyed clerk that he wasn't ready to leave just yet and needed to go back up to the psych unit. He wanted—he needed to stay longer. He couldn't explain why.

To Gregor's dismay, no one seemed to understand his plight. After a series of phone calls, and lots of head-bobbing by the clerk, Gregor was informed that he was discharged and would not be readmitted. The clerk shyly apologized. Her demeanor was infuriating. Gregor protested loudly and said he had rights. These patient rights were being violated. Security was promptly called, and Gregor was summarily dispatched off the premises by two burly security guards. He was told in no uncertain terms not to come back.

The police cruiser pulled up to the curb along the long, narrow side entrance to the hospital. A young, handsome local officer exited the vehicle and approached. Gregor had been casually lying under a large elm tree in the middle of a sprawling, well-manicured lawn adjacent to the main building on hospital property. The friendly officer approached cautiously but with a smile.

"Hi, friend. Watcha doing?"

Gregor was lying on the ground with his feet crossed and his head and neck resting on the tree trunk. He had been there for hours. He continued to chew on a twig while refusing to acknowledge the presence of the officer. He could see out of the corner of his eye that the officer was assessing the situation and surroundings. Finally, Gregor spoke.

"Minding my own business, officer. Do you mind?"

The officer replied in a soft voice. "Well, the hospital people called and—"

Gregor quickly interrupted. "So what? I'm not breaking any laws. Do you always harass law-abiding citizens?"

The officer remained composed and unperturbed. His response was calm and professional.

"Well, it's just that they're concerned. Your presence is causing alarm and concern. That in itself is a violation. But I don't want to arrest you. I just want to help. Can I give you a ride somewhere?"

"No, officer," Gregor responded curtly. "In case they haven't told you, I want to be readmitted to the psych ward, and they won't let me!"

The officer looked puzzled. "Sir, didn't they just release you from the ward earlier this morning?"

"Well, yes. But I don't feel well. I'm going to hurt myself if I don't get help."

Gregor knew the key words to say. This put the officer in a quandary, and Gregor knew it. After some thought, the officer responded.

"I talked with the hospital people just before coming here. They don't want you back. Just let me take you somewhere. Maybe to a family member or friend? I really don't want to have to arrest you."

Gregor sprang to his feet and rushed forward. He skidded to a stop three feet from the officer. It was a good thing, too. Gregory was on the brink of being tasered.

The officer was not thrilled about the idea of pumping 10,000 amps of electricity through his adversary. Luckily, he held his composure and didn't engage the trigger of the police taser gun. Gregor was not going to attack. The officer sensed that the actions before him were done out of some strange impulse, and were more reactionary than violent. The officer quickly spoke in a proactive attempt to assume control over the situation.

"C'mon pal. Let me help. Look at you. You're still wearing your hospital gown. Let me help get you dressed and cleaned up. Look at your poor bare feet. They're dirty. Let me—"

"Sir," Gregor stated with an air of annoyance, "the feet of which you speak are soiled, not dirty."

The officer grinned slightly. At that, Gregor smiled too. Suddenly it was decided that being nice to the officer was a good idea. Gregor held out his hands with the palms open and facing upward. It was a sign of passivity. Perhaps they could be friends. After all, the officer was a nice guy. He was doing his job.

The idealistic and naïve young officer would change. Of that Gregor was sure. The young man would become jaded as his career progressed. In time, he would become cynical at first. And then eventually he wouldn't care. It would benefit the officer in the long run to have that attitude. The development of the non-caring thing protects you. Gregor knew that from personal experience.

"Maybe you can help me after all," Gregor said.

Gregor decided he would allow this help from the officer. "If you truly want to help me, please sign me in via a 302 commitment. Police officers are empowered to do this if necessary. And it is necessary. I've already told you clearly and distinctly that I'm a threat to myself. These are clear grounds for admission to the psychiatric unit."

The officer scratched his head and deliberated for a while upon Gregor's words. He then shrugged his shoulders in resignation.

"Okay, I guess it's worth a try. You've sort of forced my hand here. I'll sign the 302 papers. But that doesn't mean they'll readmit you. You still have to pass the doctor interview."

"You do your part, I'll do mine, officer."

The officer reluctantly agreed. Gregor filed himself into the backseat of the police cruiser, and off they went back to the Emergency Room admissions desk.

The two men entered the ER without saying a word. The officer approached the front desk and asked the receptionist for 302 paperwork while Gregor calmly sat himself down in the waiting area. After about twenty minutes or so, the officer took the completed papers up to the receptionist for processing. He then turned and found where Gregor was sitting. He sat next to him. They were becoming friends. This made Gregor smile.

In short order, the attending ER nurse asked the men to follow her into a nearby triage room. After taking the necessary vital signs, et cetera, the nurse seated the men on iron-backed folding chairs inside the ER near the nurse's desk.

"Well, this is it. The doctor will be calling for you any minute now. Good luck on your interview."

Gregor acknowledged the officer's kind words of encouragement. A minute later, Gregor was led away to the interview room.

Some forty-five minutes later, Gregor returned. The officer hadn't moved from his seat on the iron-backed chair. Gregor took his seat next to the officer and smiled. At that instant, the officer excused himself and headed for the desk area where the attending nurse was standing in wait. Gregor watched closely. The body language was not good. The officer looked deflated as he slowly shook his head while listening to the nurse's words. After another moment, the officer returned to where Gregor was seated.

"Well … you blew it."

"Excuse me, officer?" Gregor replied with some consternation.

The young policeman looked exasperated. His face was red with frustration.

"I thought you wanted to be readmitted." The officer emphasized the word *wanted* a bit harshly. "Well, you didn't sound very 'psychotic' to the doctor. Apparently, your responses to the questions were lucid and normal. To use the nurse's term, you sounded more like a Rhodes scholar in there than somebody needing psychiatric help. I thought you knew how to handle these doctor interviews. You have to act crazy if you want admission. What the hell were you doing? Were you trying to impress the doctor with your knowledge and demeanor? What in the hell were you thinking?"

Gregor listened calmly as the officer spewed forth his frustration. He was going to say something, but the officer wasn't done venting just yet.

"You know Gregor—you beat all. Now what are we going to do? I guess I have no choice but to arrest you and put you in a cell until I can figure something else out. You obviously have no intention of helping yourself."

Of course, this was not true. Gregor prided himself on being a problem solver. He politely waited until the officer was done speaking before putting his plan into action. It was now his time to speak.

"I know you're correct, of course. My arrogance sometimes gets the best of me. A thousand pardons to you, officer." The officer just sat there shaking his head in frustration. Gregor continued. "So they want crazy do they? I'll soon rectify that problem."

The officer wasn't paying much attention to Gregor. He had his head in his hands as he contemplated what to do next. Gregor slowly rose from his seat so as not to arouse suspicion. He bent over and neatly folded up the iron-backed chair. He then quickly turned and shrieked in rage while raising the chair high above his head. The now berserk Gregor wielded the chair like an ancient warrior on attack and charged toward the nurse's station. With a savage downward blow, Gregor smashed an $8,000 heart monitor into a thousand pieces. Nurses shrieked in horror and ran away from the now insane patient. Gregor cackled in frenzied delight.

The young officer rushed quickly to subdue Gregor. As he had often done, Gregor suddenly shifted his demeanor back to being calm. This stopped the officer in his tracks. Gregor slowly unfolded the chair, and quietly sat down. He crossed his arms and gazed without emotion at the officer.

"Was that crazy enough?" Gregor asked with deadpan sarcasm.

Trying to control his look of astonishment, the officer pulled up his chair next to Gregor. Two security guards were observed in the distance, hurrying to the scene of the destruction.

"Yep, Gregor. I think that'll do it."

PSYCHO G

(PART 2)

"Hey, wait a minute! Where are you taking me? I want to stay here. What are you doing? Let me go, you big oafs."

Gregor was going to be obstinate, and the two burly security guards anticipated this. These two guys were low on brains but had biceps of steel. They were accustomed to dealing with psych patients who occasionally flew out of control. Physically, Gregor was no match for them.

"I want to see the doctor in charge. I know my rights. Unhand me, you apes."

Just then, a self-important-looking man wearing a rumpled white lab coat and carrying a clipboard entered the room. He was a slightly built, middle-aged guy who wore horned-rimmed glasses that were too large for his narrow face. His left cheek seemed to twitch involuntarily, as if an invisible gad fly were continually alighting upon his skin. "Dr. Coy" was prominently displayed on a large name plate hanging on an angle from his jacket pocket. Keeping his distance from the struggling Gregor, the doctor coldly introduced himself.

"I'm Doctor Horatio Coy, the administrative director of all psychiatric units in Cogan County."

Gregor intuitively didn't like this guy. He looked like a human weasel. People who looked that way usually took out their frustrations on others. They should never confer degrees on people like Dr. Coy. Granting them positions of power is dangerous. Even though Gregor had only observed the doctor for about thirty seconds, he had him pegged perfectly.

"Uhhh … hmmmm," the doctor cleared his throat. "Mr. errr … Gregor Schuster is it?"

Gregor didn't respond; he just glared at the bespectacled doctor.

"Well, Gregor, I've been reviewing your file. It seems you've been admitted and then readmitted to this institution in close time proximity. My files further indicate that you have been admitted to this ward on sixteen separate occasions over the past sixty months."

"Yeah … so what?" Gregor was snarling as he struggled within the clutches of the burly guards. The doctor jumped back a bit, fearful that Gregor may break free from security. When he was sure the guards would not lose their grip, the doctor continued his message to Gregor.

"Well, after careful assessment," the doctor said in high-pitched, squeaky voice, "we have decided that your manipulative patterns may not continue … at least, not at this institution. Although we are required under Psychiatric Act 303 to admit you, we are not mandated to keep you in this facility. Therefore, you will be transported forthwith to our Stallsburg facility. Best wishes for your continued mental health, Mister, errrr … Gregor."

This was the worst possible news. Gregor had made friends at this hospital. They knew him, understood him. It was difficult for Gregor to make and keep friends. Yes, this was the worst possible news. The worst possible news, indeed.

Little did Gregor know that Stallsburg Psychiatric Hospital was the Siberia of psych hospitals. It was located in an extremely remote rural area near the county line. The city of Stallsburg at one time was a prosperous coal town that flourished in the fifties and early sixties. After the coal reserves ran out, the "boom town" died. It was now a sparsely populated ghost town with limestone pollution in its water supplies. Its secondary resource—farmland—had been abandoned with the influx of the mining companies. The land subsequently was ravaged by the strip miners and was now composed of a sandy, shale-like composition that can grow nothing. Stallsburg was truly the land that time (and society) had forgotten. What a perfect place to build a psychiatric hospital. You could lock up all of the dregs of society, and nobody would notice or care. Many of the patients would acquire the traits of the town itself: abandoned, sterile, and of no use to anyone.

Gregor was loaded into the transportation van wearing arm and leg shackles. These restraints were "for his own good." There was another patient to be transported to Stallsburg. He was an incorrigible named Ralphie. Gregor had seen him before. This guy was a loose cannon who had a violent, hair-trigger temper. It never took much provocation to get him started. That's why they generally had him under heavy sedation most of the time. To Gregor's dismay, Ralphie was going to be his travel companion in the psych transportation van. To his further distress, Ralphie was not sedated. He glared at Gregor like a rabid bobcat.

The two psych patients sat across from each other. Ralphie squirmed and complained while Gregor sat calmly and quietly. A security guard took a seat next to Ralphie while another hopped behind the wheel. Lurching forward, off they all went to their destination: Stallsburg Psychiatric Hospital.

As the van spurted forward, Gregor lost his balance and fell forward. Because of the restraints, Gregor could neither regain his balance nor avoid crashing headlong into Ralphie's lap.

"Hey-hey-hey," Ralphie spouted louder and louder. "Hey, what are you doin'? Get off me." Ralphie then let out a shrill, anguished, and demented blood-curdling scream.

Gregor frantically scrambled up off of Ralphie. He rolled awkwardly to his left so as to avoid falling into the guard. This overcompensation threw him off his feet. With a sickening thud, he tumbled face-first to the floor of the van. The jarring motion of the van, combined with the limited ability to maneuver because of the shackles, made it impossible for Gregor to maintain any semblance of balance. The fact that Gregor was not the most athletic or coordinated guy around didn't help matters.

As this whole ordeal unfolded, the gruff security guard burst into uncontrollable laughter. He didn't offer Gregor any assistance back to his seat. The guard was hoping Gregor would do something awkward again. It didn't take much to amuse this Neanderthal hospital guard.

Gregor slowly inched his way back up to his knees. As he got to one foot, the slightly battered and shaken Gregor flung himself back into his seat. With a sigh of relief, Gregor tried to compose himself. After a minute, he looked up at Ralphie and smiled warmly.

"A thousand apologies, friend," Gregor offered in a conciliatory gesture.

The red-faced Ralphie glared back in annoyance.

"I don't like the way you talk, mister fancy-pants," Ralphie spouted in Gregor's direction.

The guard laughed out loud at the remark and then kept giggling. This confused Ralphie and made him more agitated. Ralphie decided the guard was taking sides. This was infuriating. Ralphie was ready to blow like a volcano. Neither Gregor nor the guard realized that he was at his tipping point and ready to explode. Were the guard and Gregor friends? Were they plotting against him?

"Again, I'm truly sorry," Gregor offered in apology.

The guard then burst into raucous laughter. That's all it took. Ralphie suddenly and unexpectedly launched himself headlong into the seated and docile Gregor. Ralphie's head collided with a violent splat into Gregor's face. The crown of the attacker's forehead shattered Gregor's nose as the cartilage cracked with a sickening crunch. Blood spurted everywhere as if being squirted out of a hose and covered both men. It looked as if they were coated by a gallon of red paint.

The guard swore out loud as he sprang into action. With his strong and hairy hands and forearms, the burly guard yanked Ralphie up by the nape of his neck. With his other arm, he grabbed Ralphie's backside and threw him back into his seat.

"Now just sit there, shit-fer-brains, and don't do that again," the guard scolded. Ralphie took this admonishment from the guard very seriously. He knew from prior experience not to disobey the guards. Ralphie just sat there but shook with a great rage.

The guard then turned his attention to Gregor. He reached down and pulled Gregor's crumpled body up by the shirt. He then unceremoniously plopped Gregor down into his seat and then started swearing.

"Sombitch, I got some of your damned blood on me, you sombitch!" The guard was mad. Real mad.

Gregor whimpered and sulked as he sat there, not daring to move or to provoke the guard into further violence. He curled up into the fetal position and played the part of the poor victim. He did not wish to provoke any more action by either of his violent travel companions, with whom he was forced to be a passenger for the next two hours. He decided he would just sit there quietly and avoid eye contact until arrival at Stallsburg.

Gregor started to daydream. He fantasized that he was an actor, and the world was his stage. "I'm so good at this," Gregor thought almost aloud. They thought he was a pathetic victim. The guard and Ralphie could believe that if they liked. He had them fooled. If they only knew the truth.

Still, Gregor could never understand why anyone would resort to violence. It was not fathomable to him. Gregor just knew deep in his heart that both men would regret their actions some day. Karma always came back to haunt such people. At least that had been Gregor's experience regarding such matters.

So Gregor just curled up and played out his part in this drama. Bright red blood flowed freely from both nostrils of his broken nose and directly into his mouth. Without thinking, he began licking at the dried, clotting fluid forming around the corners of his mouth. He then had no choice but to start lapping at the sweet red nectar as it streamed into his mouth. He gulped the sticky liquid quickly as a new pool formed almost immediately back into his cheeks. The taste of his own blood seemed to transform him, giving him more vigor and resolve. His body began coursing with strength and elation. Of course, Gregor was careful not to be observed by his travel companions. The two bullies weren't paying any attention. They were concerned only about themselves. Gregor smiled wryly to himself as he curled up even more inwardly.

Ralphie, Gregor, and the two guards arrived at Stallsburg just in time for lunch. It had been a grueling four-hour trip, at least as far as Gregor was concerned. The side door of the van slid open, and it was the first time Gregor had a chance to see the guard who had driven the van. Through the glaring sunlight, Gregor could barely make out his features. Even with the limited visibility, Gregor could tell that this guard was even fatter and hairier than his partner. How was that even possible? Gregor snickered silently to himself.

"Hey Taco, clean this butt-munch up. I don't want none of the stuffed shirts in that hospital think he got abused."

So the guard who rode in the back was named Taco—a fitting name for an obese ruffian.

"How very compassionate of you," Gregor shot back to the guard.

"Hey pal," Taco chortled. "Don't get your nose out of joint over this." Both guards then broke out into hysterics over the insensitive joke.

Meanwhile, this calamity broke Ralphie out of his daydream. The now awakened Ralphie looked ornery.

"I still don't like how you talk, you sombitch," he lashed at Gregor.

Taco gave Ralphie a thumping backhand off his temple. It immediately calmed him down.

"Hey, Bluto, give me them hand wipes in the front seat. I'll clean this butthole up real quick. I don't wanna miss lunch."

So Bluto reluctantly did as his partner requested. Not because he liked taking orders. He didn't. But only because he didn't want to miss lunch.

"Damn, you look like a raccoon," Taco said in disgust as he began wiping Gregor down with the alcohol swabs. "I hope I don't get into no trouble over this."

"What do you mean I look like a raccoon?"

Taco held up his cell phone so Gregor could see his reflection. To his amazement, Gregor noticed that both eyes were black and swollen. His nose was also horribly disfigured and leaned to one side. Taco noticed the tilted nose as well. Before Gregor could react, Taco reached out and pinched Gregor's nose like a vise between his beefy thumb and forefinger. Gregor heard cartilage crunch as Taco straightened his nose. A most intense pain shot up through Gregor's septum and into his eyes, making them water.

Taco took a minute to admire his work.

"Yeah, that looks a lot better. Here, look for yourself."

Gregor looked back at his reflection as Taco held the cellphone up. Yes, his nose had been put back into place. Maybe when the swelling went down it would look normal again. But even if it didn't, Gregor didn't care. He sort of liked the new look. His new appearance made him feel more manly.

The two burly guards led their patients through a series of wired security gates and checkpoints.

"We ain't gonna put these turds into general pop till we eat lunch. What are they havin' today?" Gregor could hear Bluto's stomach rumbling as he posed the question to the check-in person.

"Sloppy joes and fries" was the response.

"Hot damn, one of my favorites."

As the guards hustled Ralphie and Gregor into the lunchroom, Gregor couldn't help but think that Bluto probably had a lot of favorite foods. He doubted that Bluto and his partner Taco had ever missed a meal in their lives.

"You two buttholes hafta stay with us," Taco ordered. "Your paperwork ain't gonna be done till later. Don't try nuthin'. Just sit and eat and keep your pieholes shut."

"Yes, sir," Gregor said with a sarcastic smile. Ralphie just smiled too, but he wasn't happy.

The two guards feasted like slopped hogs while Ralphie and Gregor just sat there staring.

"Hey, dillhole, ain't you gonna eat your food?" Taco asked Gregor.

"No, I've got a bit of indigestion" was the deadpan reply.

"You ain't got no problem if I eat it, do you?"

Before Gregor could respond, Taco pushed Gregor's food over next to his own plate, and commenced greedily grubbing down on the second plate of food. Gregor turned his head in disgust, as

Taco actually sounded like a grunting pig when consuming the lunch.

As the guard shoved the last bite of sloppy joe into his filled cheeks, Gregor turned to Taco and said, "I'm so very glad you've eaten heartily."

He was going to say more, but suddenly Ralphie jumped up and tried to attack Gregor.

"Sombitch, I hate the way you talk," Ralphie screamed in a panicked hysteria.

Taco interceded before any damage had been done, as a couple of uniformed orderlies rushed over to see what the fuss was all about.

"Take this butt-munch to isolation till his paperwork is ready." Taco pointed to Ralphie.

The orderlies quickly escorted the protesting Ralphie away.

"This one can stay. He's my buddy."

Gregor was touched.

"Thanks, Taco. You saved me. I appreciate that," Gregor said with true feeling.

"Yeah, sure buddy. Hey, I'm gonna have dessert. You sure you don't want anything?"

"Perhaps a small cup of hot coffee would be nice."

The orderlies were directed to give Gregor the coffee as Taco began to scoff down a large piece of blueberry pie.

"May I also trouble you for a couple packs of sweetener?" Gregor asked timidly.

After the two security grunts inhaled their lunches—and every other crumb and morsel around them—they both belched almost in unison. They both laughed like hell and then pulled themselves up from the table.

"C'mon, Slappy, let's go," Bluto barked at Gregor. With a quick motion, Gregor lifted his cup, took one more small sip of his coffee and then scooted away from the luncheon table. As he did this, the guards were talking about what to do next. Apparently, they both had to go to the bathroom and were arguing as to who would go first.

"Pardon the interruption, guys," Gregor interjected. Both guards stopped talking and turned to glare at Gregor in annoyance. "I hate to bring this up, but I've lost a small medallion that had been in my possession. Apparently, it became dislodged when I was brutally attacked by Mr. Ralphie. I'm sure it's laying in the van somewhere. May we kindly retrieve the item? It has enormous sentimental value."

Bluto was incredulous and turned to Taco.

"Crissakes, Taco, you moron. Didn't you search him? They aren't allowed to have no jewelry on them."

Taco scratched his head and wondered aloud if he had indeed thoroughly searched Gregor. He then decided that he had searched him and that it was not possible for Gregor to have had a trinket in his possession.

"You better go out to the van and double-check. It's our asses if there's a trinket laying somewhere in that van. Take Spanky with you and find that damned trinket. And get back here quick. I'm going to the pisser."

Angrily, Taco grabbed Gregor by the scruff of the neck and led him through the maze of security gates and back out to the parking lot. Both men walked silently to the van, with Gregor being pushed from time to time for no apparent reason. Taco enjoyed being a ruffian and a bully.

As the morbidly obese Taco opened the side sliding door of the van, he turned to look at Gregor. He pondered entering the van himself to look around. He reconsidered. He wasn't crazy about the idea of squeezing his three-hundred-plus-pound frame into the smallish area.

"What does the damned trinket look like?"

In a meek voice, Gregor said, "It's a rather small stone, a princess cut, with an opaque ambiance and rich, chartreuse-colored hues."

Taco looked at him in feigned astonishment. "Okay, fag, you get in there and look."

The still semi-shackled Gregor was hoisted into the van by the overgrown brute. After a cursory inspection, Gregor reported that he thought he had seen a glimpse of the trinket lying wedged deep under the seat. It was stuck between the floor mat and the seat base. He couldn't reach it because of the shackles.

"Git out of the way, shit-fer-brains," Taco spouted and then pushed Gregor out of the way. "Let me see."

Gregor tumbled awkwardly out of the van as Taco squeezed his large frame into the limited space. Taco let out a sinister laugh as he saw Gregor crash to the ground. He told the "little pissant" to stay put and then aggressively began looking for the trinket. Out of frustration, he violently ripped the mat from the floor and felt around the crevices of the seat base where Gregor claimed to have seen the small stone.

"There ain't no sonofabitchin' trinket in here, you dung beetle." After uttering these words, Taco tried to back his way out of the tiny space. He was stuck. Gregor thought it was comical and quite a sight to behold. You could see the plumber's crack on Taco's butt as he lay there, struggling to get up. It would unfortunately be a vision forever etched in Gregor's brain.

When Taco finally backed his way out, he got to his feet and turned to find Gregor.

"Hey piss-for-brains, what are you doin'?"

"Ahh ... I just noticed that the gas cap needed tightening."

Gregor slowly backed away from the van. He sensed that Taco was very angry.

"I told you to stay put. Now stay away from that gas tank, you moron."

Gregor carefully backed away farther and was apologetic. Taco didn't notice the small, empty, pink paper packets blowing harmlessly away over the barren lot.

"Well, that was a damned wild-goose chase. There wasn't no trinket in that van. You're a damned troublemaker, you know that? If I wasn't in a hurry to get back home, I'd bitch-slap you all over this lot. Now get moving. We're running late."

"Truly an error on my part, kind sir," Gregor retorted to Taco's harsh words. "Thank you for checking, dear friend. I feel much better now."

Taco just stood there for a minute shaking his head.

"You are one disturbed sombitch, aren't you?"

Gregor just shrugged his shoulders and looked innocently at Taco.

"And another thing about you, boy," Taco continued. "You sure do have two lips. No wonder Ralphie wants to beat the crap outta you all the time."

Gregor gave no response.

"C'mon, let's go. I still gotta get you checked in."

Gregor was led away and back through the security gates. As much as he tried to conceal his glee, Gregor just couldn't stop grinning. He felt a warm sense of accomplishment and satisfaction inside.

News—especially bad or tragic news—spreads fast. The buzz was everywhere. Gregor first learned of the horrific and fiery crash when he overheard one of the orderlies talking to a station nurse on his assigned wing.

"It's a shame what happened to them boys the other day. Nobody deserves to die like that."

Gregor wondered what they were talking about. The chubby nurse just kept shaking her head in disbelief.

"I heard the bodies were hardly recognizable after the crash," the nurse said. The orderly nodded sadly.

"What else did you hear?"

"The van went right over the hillside at that horseshoe curve in Delmar," the orderly said. "The state police figure there was about a two-hundred-foot drop before that van hit them rocks head-on. They might've survived that, but then the police figure the van rolled a few times. Hell, they might've even survived that. But then everything ignited in flames. Them boys was trapped in there and they got cooked like holiday gooses. It's a damn shame, I tell ya."

"I heard the same thing. Do you suppose those boys were drunk? It wouldn't surprise me."

It suddenly hit Gregor like a ton of bricks. They were talking about the security guards, Taco and Bluto. Gregor was shocked and horrified by this news. It left him numb and weak in the knees. How did things like this always happen to him? Sure, those guys were ruffians and brutish. They weren't refined, nor were they professional. But heck, everybody has their faults. And Gregor was sort of attached to them. This always seemed to happen to his friends. In a moment of overwhelming self-pity, Gregor began to sob.

Then he suddenly stopped. When Gregor felt any emotion at all, it usually didn't last long before it faded into oblivion, just like those guards, fading away into oblivion. Gregor chuckled at the analogy. He then turned his attention back to the conversation.

"No, these boys wasn't drunk," the orderly said. "I heard that the engine froze up, causing the crash."

"Wasn't that vehicle safety-inspected? All of the county vehicles have to be safety-inspected on a regular basis. How does an engine suddenly seize up that belongs to the county? It doesn't make any sense."

The orderly agreed and then added, "I heard of a case one time where an engine locked up just like this one. Someone put sugar in the gas tank."

"Oh yeah, I guess that would do it. Well, there's got to be some logical explanation for it."

"Whatever happened, it sure ain't gonna bring them boys back."

Gregor walked away from the two employees. He couldn't listen to any more. He was horrified that anyone could possibly do any harm to those boys.

Those poor boys.

PSYCHO G

(PART 3)

Gregor sat on the cold iron bench, which was bolted securely to the floor for obvious reasons. He was slumped over with his head lying on his chest. This Stallsburg Psychiatric Hospital was the worst place on Earth, and it seemed like he had been here forever. Bored, miserable, and without any friends—what was a guy to do? The next 303 hearing was still a week away, which seemed like an eternity. Oh, he would act "normal" during the hearing. Gregor knew how to play the game. And they would be forced to release him shortly thereafter. By that time, he would have been here at Stallsburg for over a month. He needed to get out and could just scream out of pure frustration. They sure did work slow here in this county.

Gregor was used to being admitted to the local hospital in his neighborhood. Routines are important, and you get used to them. He had many friends on Wing 7A at his home hospital. He liked the workers, and they liked him. He knew the staff so well that when he would get admitted, it seemed like he was coming home to friends and family. But that dreaded Dr. Coy—the administrator for all of the psych units in the county—claimed to have seen through his ruse and assured Gregor he would never be admitted to his "home" again. They said he was "playing games." That was unfair. What was so wrong with sticking with familiarity?

So here Gregor sat, banished to the Siberia of all of the psychiatric hospitals, the infamous Stallsburg Psychiatric Hospital. Things didn't start out so bad for Gregor. He had met a couple of special friends en route to the facility. The transportation guards, Taco and Bluto, were a bit rough around the edges, but nobody's perfect. Gregor had formed a sort of bond with them, at least indirectly. And of course, as usual, just like anyone else who dared get close to him, they died tragically. These were yet more friends inexplicably taken from Gregor. It was so unfair. And the way these guys died was just sinister. It turned out that some disturbed soul had put sugar in the gas tank of the van in which these two fine security guards had been traveling. As they drove homeward-bound from Stallsburg, the engine seized up while the vehicle was in motion. The van careered off a steep bank and went up and over the hillside, crashing some two hundred feet below. The van caught fire, trapping the guards who were pinned inside the vehicle. They had no chance for survival and must have suffered horribly. What kind of sick human being could have put sugar in that gas tank? The thought of it all overwhelmed Gregor. Holding his head in his hands, the grieving Gregor was lost in despair and sadness.

Gregor then suddenly realized that he had been absorbed in his own emotions and was oblivious as to what was going on around him. He shouldn't have allowed that to happen. He should have known better.

"Awwww … wassa matter? Don't you feel good? Poor boy. Wassa matter?"

Gregor slowly raised his head from his hands and found himself staring directly into the hairy navel of a fleshy, partially exposed, pinkish belly. A male patient was standing within six inches, casting an ominous shadow while towering over him. This man was wearing a checkered flannel shirt. The bottom two buttons were undone. This allowed for this fellow's distended belly to protrude out as if peeking through a set of curtains. Was that belly button lint that Gregor saw? He wasn't sure, but Gregor refused to focus on the sparsely haired soft glob of flesh any further. Gregor pulled his eyes downward. He wondered who in the heck dressed this guy. Along with the checkered flannel shirt, he was sporting brightly striped, polyester bell-bottom trousers that were about four to five inches too short for his legs. How bizarre.

Suddenly, a thought struck Gregor. No—it couldn't be. But that voice ... he recognized the voice. It couldn't be. He glanced up quickly and scanned the features of the man's face. To his horror, he was correct. It was Ralphie in the flesh. The violent, raging, madman Ralphie. And he was within striking distance.

Gregor pulled back reflexively as he peered up and into the maniac's eyes. There was no sign of rage. There was not even a sign of recognition. What had they done to him? Ralphie generally viewed eye contact as a provocation, an invitation for violence. But not this time. Ralphie was heavily sedated. His eyes were blood-shot and glassy, and he was calm. He looked like a walking zombie. Gregor was annoyed by this. He wanted nothing to do with a walking zombie.

Gregor reflected back. He hadn't seen Ralphie since the two had ridden together in the same transportation van. When was that? About a month ago or so? They were both admitted to Stallsburg Psychiatric Hospital at the same time. Gregor thought that because of this commonality, they should have forged a bond of friendship. That, sadly, was not the case. Sure, Ralphie had broken and bloodied Gregor's nose and face during the trip to Stallsburg. But that was in the past. Gregor was never one to hold a grudge. "Forgive and forget" was a motto Gregor often embraced. Besides, Gregor could use a friend. He needed a friend desperately.

But this version of Ralphie was unacceptable. He wasn't fit to be a friend. Gregor gathered courage, as it was obvious Ralphie was not a threat. The institution had neutered Ralphie. They sterilized him—made him not human anymore. This repulsed Gregor. In anger, Gregor lashed out at the passive mass of carbon that stood before him.

"Get away from me. You are disgusting. Leave me alone."

Ralphie looked at Gregor as a parent would look upon a child. "Awww ... wassa matter? Don't you feel good. Awww."

Ralphie bellowed those words loudly. This din drew the attention of another psych patient meandering in the vicinity. She ambled over to investigate what the fuss was all about.

"Awww ... wassa matter?" The new visitor had a serious and compassionate look on her face but was obviously mocking Gregor while echoing Ralphie's words. Gregor stared at her in disbelief. The woman reminded him of a hag he had once seen in a very scary movie. Her hair was shockingly white, frizzy, and in complete disarray. She twitched convulsively as if she had been struck by a lightning bolt. The prematurely aged face displayed large, uneven wrinkles embedded deeply in her gray cheeks. Multiple creases and crevices were prominent on her webbed forehead. She perpetually cocked her head to one side and spoke out of the left part of her mouth, not unlike a stroke victim. She was painfully thin and frail. This was readily obvious, even though she was wearing a loose-fitting hospital gown. She reeked of both physical and mental illness. Gregor didn't want her anywhere near him. She seemed to sense this and inched closer to continue taunting the distressed Gregor.

"Wassamatter," she repeated mockingly. "Don't you feel good? Awww."

"Leave me alone, you freaks," Gregor screamed. Of course, he should have known better. His outburst just encouraged this "odd couple" to join in unison with their taunts.

"Awww," they both harmonized. They then continued in staccato fashion, "wassamatter-wassamatter-awww."

Gregor thrashed around in his seat as his tormentors escalated their verbal barrage upon him. He started shrieking loudly, which only encouraged his adversaries to scream even louder, in a contest to see who could shout loudest. As the clamor grew, it naturally drew more of the wandering psych patients over to investigate. Before he knew it. Gregor was trapped in a semicircle of maniacally grinning, mentally ill patients. There were maybe a dozen of them, all joining in a kind of tribal unity. There was nowhere to escape. When Gregor tried to get up, he'd be viciously pushed back down by the throng of excited agitators.

"Awww ... aww ... aww," this group of the insane chanted over and over again. The chants echoed loudly as they funneled through the hallways. Watching this dozen or so misfits with arms locked in unison, bellowing their mindless chant, made Gregor envision them as some kind of bizarre, otherworldly, insane chorus group from hell. They continued their relentless barrage. Some even began dancing but were careful not to break the semicircle in which Gregor was trapped.

"Awww ... awww ... awww ..." continued to cascade down from the insane voices of the frenzied mob, pelting Gregor unmercifully with the continued verbal assault. Gregor's voice was hoarse from screaming. All was lost. Gregor just pulled himself up into a tight fetal position and began sobbing uncontrollably, much to the gleeful delight of his antagonists.

At long last, the congregation of rioters parted, as two stout orderlies worked and pushed their way through the mob to get to Gregor.

"Outta the way, you morons. C'mon, move. Get the hell outta the way."

The authoritative voice of the lead orderly was adhered to by the patients. They knew better. He was the boss. If you ever crossed this guy or didn't do as he said immediately, there would be big trouble. Reflexively, the group parted and the two gruff men in white yanked Gregor up and pulled him away. Gregor was relieved and now felt safe.

"Back to the meat locker with you," the other orderly grunted in Gregor's direction. "Meat locker" referred to the solitary confinement room. He glared at Gregor with deep contempt. His lecture was not over.

"When are you gonna learn not to provoke the others? You are just a damned troublemaker. I know you act all innocent all the time, but I see right through you. You are nothing but a manipulative, psychopathic nut case."

"It takes one to know one," Gregor shot back without thinking.

The orderly lunged at Gregor but was held back by the supervising orderly.

"I'll punch your face right down through your ass, you nut job," the struggling orderly shouted while trying to break the grasp of his boss.

The supervisor lashed out at the subordinate. "What in the hell are you doing? Don't touch him. You'll get in big trouble."

"Yeah, you're right, boss. But that guy knows how to push my buttons."

Gregor then silently made a gesture in the air as if he were pushing buttons.

"See, there he goes again. You son of a ..."

The supervisor picked his partner up with his muscular arms and then body-slammed the subordinate orderly to keep him from attacking Gregor. The smaller orderly hit the marble floor with a thud and the impetus carried him into the hallway wall. The battered orderly quickly pulled himself back to his feet but was calmer, albeit slightly dazed.

"Now listen," the supervisor scolded. "He'll be rotting in solitary. It'll teach him a lesson. And if I catch you being aggressive with any of the patients again, I'm going to bust you up. Got it?"

"Yeah, boss, I got it. You are not gonna have no more trouble with me. But you gotta know, putting him in solitary ain't gonna teach him nothin'. He likes to be in solitary. It's a reward for him. He don't care about being social. He don't care about people. He thinks he's foolin' everyone. But he don't fool me. I know him. He don't care about nothin'."

Of course, the orderly was correct. Solitary confinement was preferable to mixing with those lunatics in general population. He didn't like the people here at this hospital. It was impossible for Gregor to make friends in this God-forsaken place. Gregor didn't usually have problems making friends. But it was an issue here at Stallsburg. This futility both puzzled and dismayed him.

Gregor moved over to a corner of the isolated room and sat down in sort of a lotus position. He wanted to quiet his mind and think. Introspection was important. It helped to sort things out. When you clarify things, you can figure out what is important. Sometimes, though, Gregor's mind would not cooperate. His mind would play tricks on him. Fortunately, when this happened, Gregor realized it instantly. There was the thinking Gregor, and there was the acting Gregor. When the thinking let him down, he had to resort to acting. This was necessary for self-protection.

Gregor smiled warmly. He was pleased that he knew himself so well.

For now, the thinking part was going well. So he let the thinking continue. He thought immediately of the two newest friends he had recently made. Oh my, poor Taco and Bluto. They suffered such horrible and senseless deaths. What an unexpected and tragic accident. It made no sense. Then it hit Gregor suddenly. Maybe it wasn't an accident. Is it possible they were murdered? And if so, by whom? Gregor shuddered at the thought that occurred to him next.

"I wouldn't be the least surprised if Green Man were responsible," Gregor uttered in the empty room.

It was no wonder that he thought that. Green Man had been singularly responsible for the deaths of all of his immediate family, as well as many of his closest friends. This cold-blooded, methodical serial killer had been able to escape capture by the authorities up until now. Who knew when he would resurface?

Thoughts of Green Man always shook Gregor with fear. It was time to shift focus away from those thoughts of this demon and onto something else, anything else.

Gregor then remembered reading something about serial killers in general. It was a fascinating topic. He had learned that they were psychopaths. They felt no compassion. They lacked that "caring thing" that most of us possess. They also seem to delight in the torture of others.

"Oh, that is so twisted," the disgusted and repulsed Gregor uttered in the cold, lonely room. *But oh my, were they fascinating*, he admitted to himself.

Gregor remembered that the experts claimed they could detect the traits of a serial killer in children as young as five years old. A case study of a renowned serial killer revealed that as a five-year-old, the boy would steal laboratory mice from the elementary school science laboratory. This child would insert the struggling rodent's tail into a light socket. This future murderer laughed in delight as the tiny body smoldered slowly in the boy's hands. This was a cruel and exceedingly disturbed child.

Thank God Gregor was not like that.

PSYCHO G

(PART 4)

The 303 hearing went as expected. Gregor dazzled the doctors with his brilliance. He put on quite a show and got the desired results. He was released from Stallsburg Psychiatric Hospital. It was surely time to go. He'd been there for barely more than five weeks and had experienced pure hell. This was the first time in all the psychiatric visits he'd had throughout the years that he hadn't one single friend to show for his efforts. This was the first time he hadn't had fun or felt welcome in a psych ward. Yes, it was time to go.

Stamped "lucid and highly intelligent," Gregor made his way through the security gates with his release forms in his hand. As usual, two security guards were assigned to take him home in the designated transportation van. Hmmm … maybe all of this hadn't been in vain after all. Perhaps Gregor could strike up a conversation with the guards and initiate a friendship. You never know about such things. Gregor had heard that lifelong bonds had been formed under lesser conditions.

"C'mon, you butt worm, move it."

Gregor was startled by this command, but pleasantly startled. It sounded like his old pal Taco.

"Get movin'," the voice continued. "We ain't got all day."

Gregor looked around. Was that Bluto talking?

Quickly, and to his dismay, Gregor realized that it wasn't his two old and dear friends. They had been dead for over a month now. They had been involved in a horrific accident and burned alive while trapped in their vehicle.

"Deep fried," Gregor muttered to himself, with a trace of a smile on his lips.

The two assigned guards for Gregor's trip home were named J.J. and Teddy.

"C'mon, spank master, get in the back," J.J. ordered.

"Yeah sure, no problem," Gregor responded enthusiastically. "I'm ready to go. Which one of you guys are going to sit back here with me?"

"No one is sitting back there with you. This ain't social hour. Now get in so we can get going."

Gregor was crestfallen. Did they mean that they weren't even going to try? Can't at least one of them have the decency to try to be friends with him? How unprofessional. These guys had no style. Gregor decided that these guys were not cool like Taco and Bluto. Yes, J.J and Teddy were decidedly uncool. Even their mundane names were lame.

So these two nondescript guards loaded Gregor into the back and slid the door shut. They both then hopped into the screened-off front, where Gregor couldn't even see them. The engine fired up, and the creaky old van lurched forward. Gregor was headed away from Stallsburg and onward to home. Gregor sat all alone on the bench with his legs crossed and his teeth clenched. It was no wonder that he sometimes had "attitude."

The two sharp raps on the sliding side van door startled Gregor.

"C'mon doofus, wake up. You're home," the guard named Teddy barked.

Gregor shook the cobwebs from his brain, yawned, and stretched. He couldn't believe he had been asleep for most of the four-hour trip home. As he slowly exited, Teddy gave him a sharp yank at his collar to speed him up. It caused Gregor to stumble forward and almost fall. Why were all of these guards so abusive? Was it because of the nature of their jobs? Oh, they had lots of job-related stress. That was for sure. Gregor decided he would not judge Teddy or anyone. Gregor could forgive and forget. He had shown this time and again. And with regard to Teddy, well Gregor sort of liked him. Teddy was very much like the poor deceased Taco and Bluto. And Taco and Bluto were stellar friends in every way.

"Okay, you're home, bucko. Just sign this form and me and J.J. will be on our way."

Gregor focused his eyes forward and locked in on the block numbers fastened to the three-story Victorian home before him: 114 ½ Elm Street. And sure enough, there was old Mrs. Clary peering sheepishly out the window. Mrs. Clary was a good, God-fearing Christian woman, and a decent-enough landlord. Gregor could see that she was shaking her head in disgust. She had tolerated much since the two-year lease for the vacant third-floor apartment had been signed. Gregor was informed several months ago that Mrs. Clary "rued the day" she had leased the apartment to him. The lease would expire at the end of this month. It would not be renewed.

"Hello. Earth to Greggie or whatever the hell your name is. Wake up out of your daydream and sign the damn form. We gotta get going."

"Ummm … errr … sure," Gregor responded with a start. "Hey, I've got a great idea. Why don't you and J.J. come up to my apartment for some coffee? We can sit around and talk and get to know each other better. What do you say?"

Teddy frowned with contempt.

"Not on your life, twinkle toes. Now sign the damn form."

Gregor scribbled his name on the form attached to the clipboard. With a mocking tip of the cap, Teddy spun around and headed for the driver-side door. With a "toot toot," the van sped away down Elm Street.

Gregor took a deep breath and then sighed. He turned and slowly began to walk down the concrete pathway leading to the front door. After a few steps, Gregor was finding it hard to breathe. He could feel his chest tightening with pain and anxiety, as if experiencing a heart attack. But it wasn't a heart attack. Gregor had experienced these symptoms many times before and recognized them. He was in the grip of a full-blown panic attack. Turning and running back onto the street, and sobbing uncontrollably, the quaking and quivering Gregor began shouting.

"Wait ... come back ... I don't want to be released. I need help. I need to stay with you guys. Please ... please ...," the pleading just-released patient from Stallsburg Psychiatric Hospital begged. Gregor was kneeling in the middle of the street, as if in prayer. There was no one to hear the prayers. There was no one to hear his pathetic pleas. Well, no one except for the mortified Mrs. Clary.

It was about 2:00 p.m. when a hysterical Mrs. Clary burst through the front doors of the Cogan Count Sheriff's Department. One of the assistant dispatchers rushed into the lobby to meet her. The poor woman was hyperventilating and could barely speak. The dispatcher offered her a small cup of water and encouraged her to calm down.

"Please ma'am, take a deep breath. Relax and breathe. Now then, what's the problem?"

The quivering Mrs. Clary gulped more air and then tried to speak. A dry, rasping sound was all that her vocal cords could produce. The dispatcher encouraged her to slowly sip the drink he had given her. It would soothe and lubricate the vocal cords. The woman's quivering hands took the cup and tried to reach her lips with the cool water. Because of the intense trembling, little fluid reached her lips, with most of it splattering downward onto her lap.

One of the officers assigned for evening patrol entered the lobby. "Here, let me help," Officer John Kane offered. The tall and handsome officer had a commanding presence and presented a strong and stabilizing influence on Mrs. Clary. She calmed down a bit and accepted the water from the officer's steady hands. After a few sips, she was ready to talk.

"He's going to start shooting people," she screamed rapidly. "He's a crazed madman. He's lost control. Right now, that maniac is rooting around for a rifle and ammunition. If he finds the bullets and the rifle, he'll start shooting anyone who gets in his way. That's what he said anyhow. Please stop him, stop him, somebody stop him." The pleading woman then broke down and started sobbing uncontrollably.

"Ma'am, please listen carefully," the officer said in a quiet and patient voice. "What is the address where this possible shooter is located?"

"114 ½ Elm Street," Mrs. Clary said while choking on the words. The old woman then claimed to be feeling dizzy. A second later she lay faint in the arms of the police officer.

"Summon the paramedics, quick," Officer Kane barked to the dispatcher. "And tell my partner to meet me in the front lot. Now!"

Officer Balcik pulled up in the squad car and met Kane in front of the headquarters. Kane jumped into the passenger side.

"Head to 114 ½ Elm Street, partner, and red-ball it. I'll explain on the way."

As the siren wailed and the red and blue lights whirred, Kane apprised Balcik about what was going on at 114 ½ Elm Street. Within six minutes, the patrol car arrived in the neighborhood. Balcik killed the lights and siren at Fifth and Elm so as not to alert Gregor of their arrival.

The officers cautiously exited the patrol car about three hundred feet from the 114 ½ Elm Street address and approached slowly. They could clearly hear Gregor screaming and cursing, even from that distance.

"Listen, partner," Kane said to Balcik as they continued tactically to move closer and closer to the house. "Backup will be here in a few minutes. The SWAT team is on the way too. Normally we would wait for their assistance. But my gut tells me there's a reason why this guy hasn't shot anybody yet. He's as angry as a hornet, and he's liable to do anything. But I think he can't find the gun or the ammunition. If he finds what he's looking for, then it may be too late. So I think a move has to be made now. So I'm going in. I'm ordering you not to go in with me. I'm going to try to stop him. But if I'm wrong and I walk into a trap, then only one of us gets hurt. You stay here until backup arrives. Understand?"

"Yeah, pal. I don't like it, but I understand. It makes sense."

Balcik saw the logic behind the move. He didn't want to abandon his partner, yet he had no choice but to obey the direct command of his supervisor and best friend. They embraced.

"Okay, then, here I go. One final thing—" Kane looked directly into Balcik's eyes. "If I die, tell my daughter my final words were that I love her."

"Will do, partner. But you're not going to die."

Kane turned away from Balcik and quietly opened the first-floor door to the home. He slowly crept up the squeaky stairs one at a time, hoping not to be heard by the agitated and out-of-control

Gregor. Kane heard continued banging and cursing. It sounded as if Gregor were rooting through dresser drawers and then violently slamming them shut out of frustration.

Kane believed Gregor had not found the weapon or ammunition. His earlier suspicion had been correct. He instinctively knew he had to make his move now. With a violent front thrust kick, the bedroom door seemed to disintegrate into splinters. Kane rushed in and lunged headlong from halfway across the room into the shocked Gregor. The raging madman was holding a rifle and tried to swing it around. Kane was on him too quickly. The two struggled as Kane latched onto the rifle. He vowed to himself that they'd have to pry his dead hands off the weapon before he'd release it. As the struggle continued, both men tumbled onto the queen-sized bed in the middle of the room. Neither would release his grip on the rifle.

Then, with a carefully executed *hapkido* maneuver, Kane pressed on a nerve at the base of Gregor's wrist. Gregor yowled in pain and instinctively released his grip on the rifle. Kane pried the weapon away and promptly locked the stunned Gregor into an arm bar. The officer quickly pulled out a set of handcuffs from his utility belt. He slapped the cuffs first on the left wrist and then by applying pressure, he got Gregor to submit, handcuffing the other wrist. At this point, the battle was over. Both men lay there on the bed, arm locked in arm, gasping. Gregor's breath was labored largely because he was out of shape. Kane laid there huffing because his bulletproof vest didn't allow for much expansion of the lungs.

The two prone men were stationary in this manner for a matter of minutes. Kane finally gulped a large amount of oxygen and was able to announce "Code 4" into his walkie-talkie. A wave of blue uniforms led by Officer Balcik then stormed the room, being assured that all was secure. They all stopped and looked on in astonishment at the two gasping men lying on the bed with arms locked.

"Aw, ain't this sweet? I hope we ain't disturbing you lovebirds," the commanding sergeant snickered. Everyone laughed—even Kane and Gregor.

"Okay, now what do we do with him?"

Officer Kane's supervisor seemed to ponder this question for a moment. "Let's just 302 commit him for now. He's definitely a threat to himself and others. In the meantime, we'll contact the district attorney's office and figure out what charges to file."

"Okay, Sarge," Kane replied. "I'll run him up to the hospital and get that done. And when his hearing comes up in about a week, we'll have the arrest warrants ready."

"Right," the sergeant agreed.

To Gregor's absolute delight, he was informed that he would be committed at the local hospital. He was going home. He couldn't have been happier.

"Nine-four-four."

"Nine-four-four," Officer Kane responded.

"Ten-nineteen, ten-twelve," the dispatcher ordered.

"Ten-four," Officer Kane replied. He wondered who was at the station requesting to speak to him. Well, he'd find out soon enough. He was only five minutes away.

Kane entered headquarters through the designated "police only" entrance and proceeded to the front lobby. A seated gentleman was awaiting his arrival. When Kane glanced through the bulletproof glass to observe the visitor, his jaw dropped in disbelief. There was Gregor, sitting there calmly, reading a magazine. How was this possible? He was admitted to the psych ward two days ago. How did he get out? There hadn't been a rush to obtain the arrest warrants. The police and district attorney thought they had plenty of time to write them up. Well, they were wrong. Kane thought he'd better act quickly.

"Sully, come here." The dispatcher quickly moved over to see what Kane wanted. "Notify Sergeant O'Malley immediately. Then contact the DA's office. We need those arrest warrants *now*. I'll stall this Gregor guy until I hear further instructions."

"Okay, Kane, right away," the dispatcher replied, acknowledging the gravity of the situation.

Kane slowly opened the lobby door and entered, smiling warmly at Gregor as he looked up from his magazine. Gregor had an annoyed look on his face.

"Hi, Gregor. What's up? How are you doing?"

"Salutations, Officer Kane. I'm doing swimmingly. Thank you."

"Soooo … I thought you were supposed to be at the hospital for a while. Well, you're not there. Why is that?"

Gregor's annoyed grimace turned into a full-blown scowl.

"Because that damned administrator Dr. Coy kicked me out. He said something about being sick of babysitting me. He didn't care that the police signed me in. He said I was your problem, not his. So they just simply released me. This is quite a glitch in the system, don't you think?"

Kane looked around nervously. Why hadn't anyone gotten back to him yet? What did the DA want him to do? Where were those damned warrants?

"So what do you want to do, my friend?" Kane wasn't sure what else to say to the volatile man sitting next to him.

"Officer Kane, first of all, thank you for your courtesy regarding this most perplexing dilemma. Now, to the point of the matter. The purpose of my visit is to ask you a question. I need the vital information only you can provide."

"Okay, Gregor," Kane responded with some trepidation. "What is your question?"

"Well, as you know, some forty-eight hours ago, you viciously attacked me. You rendered me helpless by disarming me from my rifle. By the way, I hold no grudge toward you and your valorous act. But back to the point. As you know, the rifle had no ammunition in it. It was a .30-06 rifle, and I was erroneously trying to insert .30-30 shells into it. This mistake will not occur again; this I can assure you."

"Gee," Officer Kane said in reply in an attempt to stall for time. "I would hope you wouldn't do that, Gregor."

"Officer Kane," Gregor snapped, "please allow me to finish."

Officer Kane shrugged his shoulders and nodded his assent for Gregor to continue.

"So my question to you is this, Officer Kane: The next time you are dispatched to my home, I'll have a loaded rifle poised and ready to go. What will you do if I point that rifle at you?"

Officer Kane's jaw tightened. He looked earnestly into Gregor's eyes. The insane man looked back unblinking.

"I'll shoot you to kill you," Officer Kane said with a mixture of resolve and sadness.

"Aha! Just as I suspected. Very good, and thank you," Gregor responded with a satisfied smile. "I'll be on my way."

Officer Kane thought he had heard it all in his fifteen years' experience on the force. This "suicide by cop" threat was a first.

As Gregor got up to leave, Officer Kane grabbed him by the arm. "Wait a minute. You can't just leave on that note. I answered your question. Now you answer one of mine."

"Very well, Officer Kane. Quid pro quo."

Officer Kane looked pleadingly into Gregor's eyes. "Why? Why would you put me in that position? I don't want to shoot you. I don't want to shoot anyone. Why would you put me in that position? I would have to live with that for the rest of my life."

Gregor glared at Officer Kane with true incredulity. "Officer Kane. I'm appalled. This isn't about you. Quit being selfish. It's about me. I may want to die soon. Now I am clear as to how to facilitate that goal. Now please, Officer Kane, I must leave without delay. I am late for an appointment. Good day, sir."

Just then Officer Balcik entered the lobby. The look on his face offered no encouragement as Gregor strode out the front door.

"John, let him go. We have to let this guy walk for now." Officer Kane sat back down dejectedly. "The warrants won't be ready for another three hours. When we get them, we'll pick this Gregor guy up. Our hands are tied for now."

"For God's sake, we can't let this maniac just walk out of here," Kane said to his partner. "What the hell is going on? First the hospital lets him out on some kind of vindictive technicality. And now the warrants aren't ready. Society needs to be protected from this guy. How do we stand by and let this guy walk away?"

"It's called protecting his rights and due process and all of the rest of that happy horseshit. The bottom line is we gotta let him go. Don't worry, we'll pick him up in a few hours. C'mon pal. Let's go get a cup of coffee. We'll have Gregor behind bars before our shift ends today."

At last the warrants arrived at the police station. Officers Balcik and Kane raced down to 114 ½ Elm Street to serve them forthwith. "It's about time these damn warrants were delivered," Kane said. Balcik just nodded his head in agreement as he wove through traffic in the wailing patrol cruiser. The officers bailed out of the police car upon arrival and sprinted to the door at 114 ½ Elm Street.

"'Where's Gregor?' Gee, officers, you missed him by about half an hour," Mrs. Clary told the eager policemen.

"Did he mention where he was going?"

"Why, heavens, yes. He was very adamant about catching the last bus of the day, up to Stallsburg. He mentioned something about paying a visit to an old friend named Ralphie. He had unfinished business up at Stallsburg and doesn't like loose ends when it comes to business. Gregor made a promise to himself as a child to always tie up loose ends."

"What were his words exactly?"

"Well, let's see … Oh, yes. He said he was going to finish what he started."

RALPHIE

With a great deal of trepidation,...Gregor waited. The patients' return from the asylum was imminent. Why can't they keep the "Ralphies" of the world locked up? They protect us from the Mansons much better than they do the "Ralphies". It's not that Gregor was nervous. He never showed that. It's just that, when in darkness, the incessant fluttering of his hands was manically obsessive.

Sigh-there it was-the inevitable rapping at the door. The sound of creaky hinges. Then the swollen shadow, growing...spreading... ever so ominously. Closer. Closer.

The frozen grin, painted on a twisted face. Voila. Enter Ralphie...stage left.

Adorned in a gilded brocade jacket, which was accented with a peacock colored faux fur neck warmer, Ralphie sashayed over to the near corner as if he were a Chilean fashion model.

"How do you like it? I'm just crazy for all these lush textures," he gushed.

———

"Well Ralphie, I see the electro-shock therapy treatments have done wonders for your disposition."

"Indubitably, kind sir," Ralphie replied while curtseying.

This was a real 'head scratcher'. Gregor hadn't expected to see a different Ralphie. This was a docile Ralphie. This was a benign Ralphie.

As if that mattered, Gregor silently mused.

Ralphie edged closer to Gregor. With his head slightly cocked, he inspected Gregor from a safe distance.

"Hey guv'nor," Ralphie said with a mock cockney voice, "… don't I know you?"

"What do you think-my fine feathered friend?"

"Ahhh…the game is afoot," Ralphie squealed with glee. "Hmmm…who art thou whom beckons me, I do pray?"

"C'mon Ralphie…think. We go way back."

Gregor then changed the inflection in his voice to that of a southern drawl. "Git them thar neurons a firin pardner. Who am I?"

Ralphie inched closer. His inspection of the strange visitor now demanded his full concentration. Suddenly, like a bolt, a look of recognition flashed onto Ralphie's face.

"Eureka!" Ralphie shouted. "It's you. I knew it."

With a self-assured smile, Gregor felt some pride in helping Ralphie recover this dormant memory.

"Tony-it's you. I missed you. Oh, Tony. Tony, Tony, Tony."

"Noooo," Gregor shrieked. "Wrong…Gunga-Din."

"No, I know it's you Tony. Tony, my boss. Tony my boss man. Tony, Tony, Tony."

It suddenly came 'crashing in' on Gregor yet again, about how annoying Ralphie can be. Why did Ralphie always have to 'best him' all the time?

Ralphie began to dance. It was more of a shuffle. It resembled a very ill man performing the Irish jig. Next, came the singing.

"*Tony, Tony, bow boney; banana flanna foe foney; fee fie foe floney….Tony.*"

"Ralphie, stop it," Gregor scolded.

Ralphie continued, unheeded and unabated.

After a few more moments, the unflappable Gregor decided to use his superior wit to quell this theatrical specter of the absurd.

"Ralphie, remember-I'm your boss. I'm ordering you to cease and desist. At once."

Ralphie stopped in his tracks, and looked sheepishly at Gregor.

"I'm sorry Tony. I didn't mean no disrespect Tony. Are we friends again Tony Baloney? Please Tony Baloney. Please Tony Baloney. Please…"

"Enough of this banter you miscreant," Gregor interrupted. Ralphie immediately fell into complete silence.

With the now almost deafening silence, Gregor was able to reflect on what had just happened. He was proud of the way he had just conducted himself. Gregor never lost control…well almost never. And on the rare occasions that he did, he'd always quickly recovered. Superior intellect and emotional control was always the key. My, how others must've envied him.

The self-congratulatory accolades could wait, Gregor decided. It was time to concentrate on the task at hand. Gregor strained while reaching for the small package implanted firmly upon a cavernous compartment on his person. He removed a small glass vial. After examining the contents closely, Gregor deftly unscrewed its small cork top, and poured the few drops of clear liquid into his iced tea.

"Watcha putting in that there drink?" Ralphie asked this in the same southern drawl that Gregor had used earlier. "It's sweetener…aint it? I'm a hankerin for something to guzzle pardner. I'd be much obliged if you'd let me mosey on up to the bar and have a swig of that there sasperilla."

"Oh heavens no," Gregor said in admonishment. "Kind sir, it would be unwise to partake in this liquid refreshment that has now been augmented by the nectar of the gods. It may not agree with your constitution."

These words only titillated the eager Ralphie into a bit of a frenzy.

"I'll summon a servant to fulfill your request for refreshment," Gregor offered helpfully. "Please excuse me. I won't be a moment."

Ralphie nodded his assent with a wide-eyed and impish grin.

Gregor bowed formally, not unlike a Buddhist monk, and hastily departed.

Gregor returned in short order, with an icy drink in his hand. This delightful lemony flavored brew would surely quell the thirst of his good buddy Ralphie.

"I'm back," Gregor announced excitedly. "Look what I've got you little…"

Gregor dropped the drink and gasped in horror. An aspirating Ralphie was lying on the floor, twitching spastically like a freshly caught fish out of water. Gregor was incredulous. This couldn't be happening…again. Yet, there it was-right before his very eyes.

Gregor rushed to his fallen friends' side, and tried to calm him. He gently stroked Ralphie's hair while carefully watching the shallow rise and fall of the stricken man's chest. The breaths were becoming more raspy and faint. What was Gregor to do? He wasn't a doctor. He decided to continue to do what he did best. He nurtured Ralphie. He sang to Ralphie. He helped ease Ralphie's pain by stroking his temples.

With a final gurgling sound, the breathing stopped. Gregor continued to hold Ralphie as he gazed lovingly into Ralphie's vacant lifeless eyes. A look of peaceful contentment was frozen on Ralphie's face.

Gregor flew into a jealous rage. Why did Gregor always have to shoulder the burden of others? Why was a sense of peace so elusive for him, yet so easily attained by others? This was Gregor's cross to bear. It was a curse to always be so strong.

The proper authorities would be promptly notified. They'd be of no help…of course. The official cause of death was determined to be "unknown". Why were the law enforcement officials always so clueless? Gregor knew who was responsible for Ralphie's death. Would anybody listen to what he had to say? No-of course not.

Gregor tried to fight the emotions…but they overtook him. He was grief-stricken. Why did these things always happen to him? Why was he always the victim? He sobbed hysterically… for perhaps twenty seconds. He then abruptly stopped. He loved how he was so in touch with his emotions. He admired that in himself. He loved how he was connected to his feelings. It made him human. He was not a monster like that heinous serial killer-Green Man.

Where would Gregor go? What would he do…now that another of his friends was savagely taken from him? There was only one thing "to do". After all, Gregor had to admit to some culpability regarding the death of Ralphie. Apparently, he had unwittingly led Green Man blindly to yet another of his friends.

What a twisted mind this Green Man had. Systematically, this killer had taken everything and everyone important in Gregor's life. Sooner or later, he'd claim Gregor as his final triumph. Gregor wasn't going to go down without a fight. It was now time for the hunter to become the hunted.

What choice was there? Gregor would formulate a plan…a plan to ensnare the cunning Green Man. But what then? Gregor was passive and non-violent. He was no killer. How would he effectively deal with so ruthless a demon as Green Man?

Gregor would use his superior intellect. He'd find a way to settle the score. It was payback time. Green Man would finally feel the wrath of Gregor. It was time for Gregor to finish what Green Man had started.

END

Printed in the United States
By Bookmasters